An Island in the Sun

Written *by* Stella Blackstone
Illustrated *by* Nicoletta Ceccoli

I spy with my little eye a bird flying by.

I spy with my little eye the sun in the sky and a bird flying by.

I spy with my little eye a dolphin jumping free and the sun in the sky and a bird flying by.

I spy with my little eye an island far from me and a dolphin jumping free and the sun in the sky and a bird flying by.

I spy with my little eye a big tangly tree on an island far from me

and a dolphin jumping free and the sun in the sky and a bird flying by.

I spy with my little eye a beach beside the sea and a big tangly tree on a island far from me and a dolphin jumping free and the sun in the sky and a bird flying by.

I spy with my little eye someone waiting for me on a beach beside the sea

and a big tangly tree on a island close to me and a dolphin jumping free

and the sun in the sky and a bird flying by.

Together we laugh, together we play, together we fish 'til the end of the day.

What did I spy with my little eye?

And shall we sail home now, just you and I?

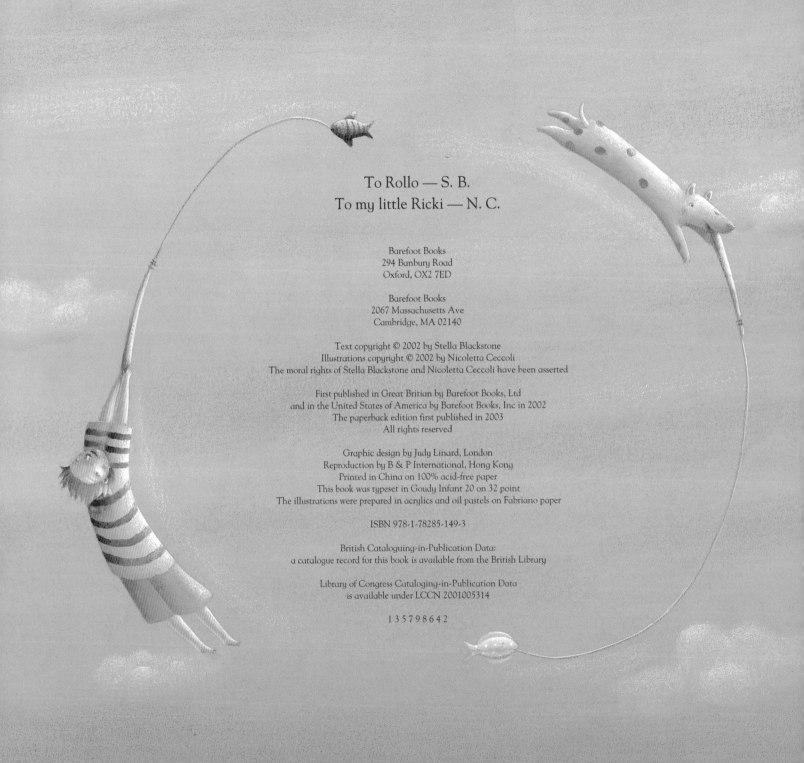

To Rollo — S. B.
To my little Ricki — N. C.

Barefoot Books
294 Banbury Road
Oxford, OX2 7ED

Barefoot Books
2067 Massachusetts Ave
Cambridge, MA 02140

Graphic design by Judy Linard, London
Reproduction by B & P International, Hong Kong
Printed in China on 100% acid-free paper
This book was typeset in Goudy Infant 20 on 32 point
The illustrations were prepared in acrylics and oil pastels on Fabriano paper

ISBN 978-1-78285-149-3

British Cataloguing-in-Publication Data:
a catalogue record for this book is available from the British Library

Library of Congress Cataloging-in-Publication Data
is available under LCCN 2001005314

1 3 5 7 9 8 6 4 2